JEROME
the Babysitter

Eileen Christelow

Clarion Books

TICKNOR & FIELDS: A HOUGHTON MIFFLIN COMPANY

New York

For Allan

Clarion Books
Ticknor & Fields, a Houghton Mifflin Company
Copyright © 1985 by Eileen Christelow

Library of Congress Cataloging in Publication Data

Christelow, Eileen.
Jerome the babysitter.

Summary: Mrs. Gatorman's nine frisky little
pranksters put Jerome, their baby sitter, through
his paces.
1. Children's stories, American. [1. Alligators—
Fiction. 2. Baby sitters—Fiction] I. Title.
PZ7.C4523Je 1985   [E]   84-12738
PA ISBN 0-89919-520-2

Y 10 9 8 7 6 5 4 3

It was five days before allowance day and Jerome
was broke.

"I can't even buy an ice cream cone," he sighed.

"Go find a job," said his older sister, Winifred,
who was a babysitter. "Then you'll be rich like me."

Sometimes Winifred had so many babysitting jobs, she asked her friend Lulu to help.

"You should ask me to help," said Jerome. "I'd be a terrific babysitter."

"You're too young," said Winifred.

"Why don't you go sell lemonade?" said Lulu.

"But I want to be a babysitter," said Jerome.

"Brothers are such pests!" sighed Winifred.

Just then someone called who needed a babysitter right away.

"Oh no," groaned Winifred. "It's Mrs. Gatorman!"

"Don't look at me," Lulu said. "I'm busy!"

"I'm not busy," said Jerome.

"What a wonderful idea!" said Winifred.

"After this, he'll never ask to babysit again," whispered Lulu.

"Oh boy," said Jerome. "You're a real peach Winifred!" He hopped onto his bike and hurried over to the Gatorman house.

Mrs. Gatorman rushed out of the front door as soon as Jerome arrived.

"I'm late!" she said. "The little angels are eating their supper. All you have to do is put them to bed."

"That sounds easy," said Jerome.

Then he heard a loud crash. "What was that?" he asked.

"I didn't hear a thing," said Mrs. Gatorman as she jumped into her car. "Good luck, Jerome. I'll be back in a couple of hours."

Jerome found the Gatorman kids in the kitchen.
They did not look like little angels.

Jerome gulped. "I'm Jerome, the babysitter," he
said.

"Oh good! A NEW babysitter!" said the Gatorman
kids.

One of them offered Jerome a piece of candy from
a heart-shaped box...

...FULL OF FROGS!

"Yipes!" gasped Jerome, as one of the frogs
jumped onto his head.

"April fool!" cried the Gatorman kids.

"This isn't April Fools' Day!" said Jerome.

"It's always April Fools' at our house," said the kids. "You look a little shaky. Would you like to sit down?"

They offered Jerome a chair...

...WITHOUT A SEAT!

"Oh no!" groaned Jerome.

"We fooled you again!" said the Gatorman kids.

"Well you won't fool me a third time!" said Jerome. "I'm going to give you a bath and put you to bed."

He marched the Gatorman kids into the bath-
room and filled the tub with water. The Gatorman
kids filled it with bubblebath.

"Don't put in too much," said Jerome.

"That's way too much!" shouted Jerome.
"All I can see is bubbles! Where are you?"
The Gatorman kids had vanished.

Jerome searched all over the house. He couldn't find them anywhere.

"Winifred should have warned me about this," he grumbled. Then he opened the coat closet door.

Four alligators walked out. They were dressed in hats and coats.

"Who are you?" gasped Jerome.

"Just the visiting relatives," they said.

"Excuse me!" said Jerome. "I was looking for the Gatorman kids."

"Maybe they're up on the roof," suggested the relatives.

"I hadn't thought of looking there," said Jerome.

One of the relatives found a ladder and held it
while Jerome climbed up.

No one was on the roof...

...but someone was taking
the ladder away.

"See you later, alligator!"
shouted the Gatorman kids.

"Hey wait! Come back here!"
yelled Jerome.

But they ran into the house,
leaving him stranded on
the roof.

"I'll never get down," groaned Jerome. "What will
Mrs. Gatorman say if she finds me up here?"

Then he heard a whistle. A policeman was stand-
ing on the sidewalk, pointing at him.

"Stop thief!" yelled the policeman.

"Who me?" gasped Jerome. "I'm not a thief!"

"That's a likely story," said the policeman as he hauled Jerome down from the roof.

"But I'm babysitting the Gatorman kids," said Jerome.

"The Gatorman kids!" said the policeman. "I've heard about them. You better get back to work."

After the policeman left, Jerome peeked through
a window. The kids were watching a monster movie
on T.V. They looked scared.

That gave Jerome an idea.
A few minutes later...

...he knocked on the window.

The Gatorman kids looked up.

"It's the monster!" they screamed.

"Go to bed!" snarled the Monster. "Or I'll come in and get you!" He started to raise the window.

The Gatorman kids raced to their bedroom.

They jumped into bed and hid under the covers.
Then they heard footsteps.

"The monster is coming to get us!" they all
screamed.

The bedroom door opened slowly.

"April fools!" said Jerome.

When Mrs. Gatorman returned home, she found
Jerome reading bedtime stories to the children.

"I don't believe it!" she said. "The little devils are
almost asleep. How did you do it?"

"Uh...er...it was easy," said Jerome.

Mrs. Gatorman paid Jerome.

"You obviously know more about babysitting than your sister, Winifred," she said. "The last time she babysat, I found her on the roof."

"You did?" said Jerome.

When Jerome got home, Winifred and Lulu were waiting for him.

"How did you like babysitting at the Gatormans?" Winifred asked.

Lulu giggled.

"The kids were little angels," said Jerome.

"They were?" said Winifred.

"Oh yes," said Jerome. "And here's a present to thank you for giving me such a wonderful job."

He handed Winifred a heart-shaped box...

...FULL OF FROGS!